THE
Little
Hummingbird

MICHAEL NICOLL YAHGULANAAS

with a message from Wangari Maathai

THE
Little
Hummingbird

GREYSTONE BOOKS

Vancouver/Berkeley

To the Indigenous peoples of East Africa,
the South American Altiplano,
and the Northern Pacific Islands—you,
who have done so much for so long.

MNY

HERE is the story

of the great forest

that caught on fire.

The terrible fire raged and burned.

All of the animals were afraid and fled from their homes. The elephant and the tiger ran. The beaver scurried and the frog leapt away.

Above them the birds flew in a panic.

The creatures huddled at the edge
of the forest and watched.

All except for one.

Little Hummingbird did not abandon
the forest. She flew as fast as she could to
the stream. She picked up a single drop
of water in her beak.

Little Hummingbird flew back and let the water fall onto the ferocious fire.

She dashed to the stream and brought another drop, and she continued, back and forth, back and forth.

The other animals watched Little Hummingbird, and they were frightened.

"What can I do?" sobbed Rabbit.
"This fire is hot, and I am scared."

"This fire is so big," howled Wolf,
"and I am so small."

"I can't do anything about this fire,"
croaked Frog.

"My wings will burn!" cried Owl.

Little Hummingbird continued her work.
She flew quickly, picking up more water
and putting it, drop by drop, onto the
burning forest.

Finally, Big Bear said, "Little Hummingbird, what are you doing?"

Little Hummingbird looked at the other animals. She said, "I am doing what I can."

DO THE BEST YOU CAN

A MESSAGE FROM

Wangari Maathai

NEARLY THIRTY years ago I planted seven trees in Kenya, Africa. Since then I have worked with thousands of others who have planted more than thirty million trees. We have shared our important work with people in other countries in Africa and around the world.

One of the greatest lessons I have learned is that all people—young or old, big or small, girl or boy—have power. We can achieve the life we want for ourselves and our families when we pay attention to protecting our environment. We must not wait for others to do it.

Many years ago I learned the practice of not wasting resources but instead using them with respect and gratitude. I also practice the Four Rs: Reduce, Reuse, Repair, and Recycle.

We can practice the Four Rs wherever we live, whether we are rich or poor, or live in the country or the city. For me, this means continuing to plant trees, particularly now that the long rains have come to Kenya. I also call

on my colleagues to ensure that we print on both sides of each sheet of paper so that we can reduce the amount we consume. And I urge everyone to avoid plastic bags that are used once then thrown away.

These are just a few examples. You can do many other small things that will make a difference in your home, your neighborhood, and your country.

We sometimes underestimate what we can accomplish, but there is always something we can do. Like the little hummingbird, we must not become overwhelmed, and we must not rest. Today and every day, dedicate yourself to appreciating nature and to protecting your home and the world's resources. We can all be like the little hummingbird, doing the best we can.

THE AMAZING

HUMMINGBIRD

HUMMINGBIRDS are amazing. Not only are they beautiful, they can also fly up to 50 kilometers (31 miles) per hour and hover in midair by flapping their wings more than 50 times per second. And they are the only birds able to fly backwards.

More than 350 species of this extraordinary little bird live on earth, all in the Western Hemisphere. The hummingbird appears in the stories of many peoples, including the parables of the indigenous peoples of South, Central, and North America.

The hummingbird often symbolizes beauty and agility, as well as hope. This story of a small hummingbird determined to put out the forest fire is told by the Quechua people of Ecuador and Peru. The Tsimshian people of the North Pacific describe the hummingbird as a joyful messenger. If she appears during a time of sorrow or pain, they know that healing will soon follow.

The hummingbird is often thanked for bringing life-giving rain. In a story from the Pueblo people of the southwestern United States, a hummingbird gathers clouds from the four directions in order to bring rain to douse the flames that are burning the earth.

In the language of the Haida Nation of the North Pacific, the hummingbird is called *dukdukdiyahm*, in imitation of the delicate bird's song and the sound of its beating wings.

Little Hummingbird in the burning forest and the hummingbirds in the stories of many peoples show us that it is not always the largest or the loudest that can do the most good. Little Hummingbird's efforts are a reminder that the one who is not afraid to act can make the biggest difference.

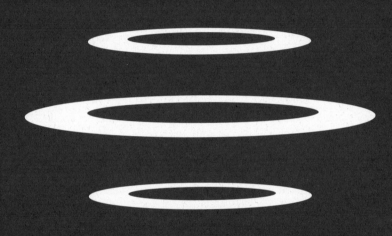

Greystone Books Ltd.
www.greystonebooks.com

Cataloguing data available from Library and Archives Canada

ISBN 978-1-55365-533-6 (cloth)
ISBN 978-1-55365-913-6 (epub)

Cover and text design by Jessica Sullivan,
Naomi MacDougall, and Nayeli Jimenez
Printed and bound in China by 1010 Printing International Ltd.

Canada

We gratefully acknowledge the financial support of the Canada Council
for the Arts, the British Columbia Arts Council, the Province of British
Columbia through the Book Publishing Tax Credit, and the Government
of Canada through the Canada Book Fund for our publishing activities.

Greystone Books is committed to reducing the consumption of old-growth
forests in the books it publishes. This book is one step towards that goal.

MICHAEL NICOLL YAHGULANAAS challenges stereotypes through illustrated storytelling, drawing on his Haida background. His books include *A Tale of Two Shamans*, *The Last Voyage of the Black Ship*, *Flight of the Hummingbird*, and the graphic novel *Red*. He has exhibited in major galleries including the Bill Reid Gallery, the McMichael Gallery, UBC's Museum of Anthropology, the Glenbow Museum, and the National Arts Centre. His Haida anime "Flight of the Hummingbird" can be viewed on YouTube. www.mny.ca

WANGARI MAATHAI is the founder of the Green Belt Movement, an environmental organization that provides income, education, and sustenance to millions of people in Kenya through the planting of trees. Maathai is also an environmental activist, an advocate for civil society and women's rights, and a parliamentarian. She has been honored with numerous awards, including the Nobel Peace Prize. She has written three books: *The Challenge for Africa*, *Unbowed: A Memoir*, and *The Green Belt Movement*. www.greenbeltmovement.org